MONKEY'S MARCHING BAND

by Michaela Muntean · pictures by Nicole Rubel

Dial Books for Young Readers

E. P. Dutton, Inc. New York

Monkey loved marching bands, and more than anything else, he wanted to play in one.

But where do you begin when you want to play in a marching band? "I would begin with one sound," said Monkey. "One big sound from one big bass drum."

So Monkey strapped a bass drum around his neck and went off down the street, beating his drum and marching in time to its *boom, boom, boom* beat.

Find the card with the picture of the bass drum. Put it on the box with the number **1**.

Zebra heard the sound of the drum.

"I think it's the beginning of a
marching band!" he cried.
And he ran outside with his cymbals
and stepped in time behind Monkey.

Boom, boom, boom, sounded Monkey's
big bass drum.
Crash, crash, crash, answered Zebra's
gleaming cymbals.

Find the card with the picture of the cymbals.
Put it on the box with the number **2**.

From her window Tiger saw Monkey and
Zebra marching down the street.
"It's a two-piece marching band," she
said. "But my trumpet would make it three!"
So Tiger ran outside and joined the parade.
Toot, toot, toot, she played on her trumpet.

Find the card with the picture of the trumpet.
Put it on the box with the number **3**.

The music woke Lion from his nap.

"My piccolo would sound great with
that marching band!" he said.
And off he went to join the line,
playing a sweet *tweet, tweet*
on his long, shiny piccolo.

Find the card with the picture of the piccolo.
Put it on the box with the number **4**.

Giraffe was eating lunch when she heard
the music of the marching band.

"They need my trombone," she said.
So Giraffe ran to join the parade.
She stepped in line behind Lion, sliding
her long trombone, *waah, waah, waah,* in
time to the beat of the drum and the crash of
the cymbals and the *toot, toot, toot* of
the trumpet and the *tweet, tweet, tweet*
of the piccolo.

Find the card with the picture of the trombone.
Put it on the box with the number **5**.

Baboon was standing outside his house when the parade rounded the corner.

"What a lovely marching band!" he cried. "But they are missing that big, deep sound only a tuba can make."

So Baboon got in line with his tuba and blew a deep *oomp-pah-pah* in time to the other instruments.

Find the card with the picture of the tuba.
Put it on the box with the number **6**.

Ostrich sat right up when she heard that marching band.

"A snare drum is the sound it needs!" she said. So off she ran to join Monkey's marching band with the *rat-tat* beat of her little snare drum.

Find the card with the picture of the snare drum.
Put it on the box with the number **7**.

Crocodile saw the marching band
from his island in the river.
He swam to shore as fast as he could
and ran to get his xylophone.
Then he joined the parade behind Ostrich,
playing *ping-pong-bong* on his xylophone.

Find the card with the picture of the xylophone.
Put it on the box with the number **8**.

Rhinoceros smiled when she heard the music.

"There's one more sound that marching band needs," she said, "and I know what it is!" So Rhinoceros brought up the rear of the parade, playing *ding, ding, ding* on her triangle.

Find the card with the picture of the triangle.
Put it on the box with the number **9**.

And Monkey was happier than he had ever been.
Because he was leading a real marching band,
stepping in time with the other musicians,
and filling the streets with music.

Now turn all the cards over, one by one,
to make a surprise picture.